POSTCARDS · FROM ·

India

Denise Allard

RSVP

RAINTREE STECK-VAUGHN
PUBLISHERS
The Steck-Vaughn Company

Austin, Texas

Published by Raintree Steck-Vaughn Publishers, an imprint of Steck-Vaughn Company

A ZOË BOOK

Editors: Kath Davies, Pam Wells
Design: Sterling Associates
Map: Julian Baker
Production: Grahame Griffiths

Library of Congress Cataloging-in-Publication Data

Allard,Denise. 1952-
   India / Denise Allard.
      p. cm. — (Postcards from)
   Includes index.
   ISBN 0-8172-4027-6 (hardcover). — ISBN 0-8172-6222-9 (softcover)
   1. India—Description and travel—Juvenile literature. I. Title. II. Series.
DS414.2.A52 1997
915.4—dc20
                                      95–52955
                                         CIP
                                         AC

Printed and bound in the United States

2 3 4 5 6 7 8 9 0 WZ 04 03 02 01 00

Photographic acknowledgments

The publishers wish to acknowledge, with thanks, the following photographic sources:

Brian Warriner - cover r; / Gina Corrigan - title page; / N.A.Callow 10; / Tony Gervis 12 / David Beatty 26; / Robert Harding Picture Library; The Hutchison Library - cover tl; / Michael MacIntyre - cover bl; / Juliet Highet 6; / Material World 8; / Maurice Harvey 12; / Patricio Goycoolea 16; Impact Photos / Ben Edwards 18; / Christopher Cormack 20, 24; / Jean Hitchings 22; / Alain Everard 28.

The publishers have made every effort to trace the copyright holders, but if they have inadvertently overlooked any, they will be pleased to make the necessary arrangement at the first opportunity.

Contents

All the words that appear in **bold** are explained in the Glossary on page 30.

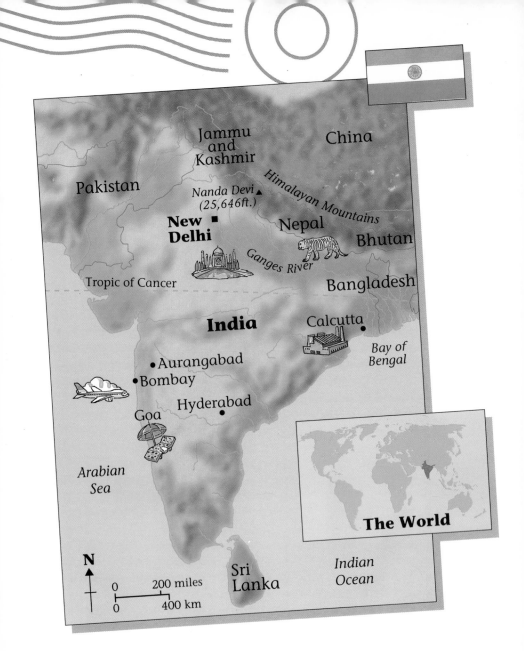

A big map of India
and a small map of the world

Dear Carol,

India is a long way from home. The plane took more than 14 hours to fly to India from New York. You can see India in red on the small map. India is a very big country.

Love,

Kim

P.S. Dad says the United States is almost three times bigger than India. About 853 million people live here.

The Red Fort, one of the most famous old buildings in Delhi

Dear Sandra,

New Delhi is the **capital** city of India. There are many tall buildings and parks here. The streets are full of people, buses, and other noisy **traffic**. It is a very busy city.

Love from,

Becky

P.S. Mom says that most people in India speak a language called Hindi. Hindi writing looks different from English writing. Many people also speak and write English.

Fresh vegetables for sale at a village
market, near the Ganges River

Dear Adam,

We went out for lunch today. I had rice with vegetables. The vegetables were cooked in a hot sauce called *curry*. Mom paid for the meal with Indian money called *rupees*.

Love,

Kristy

P.S. Dad says that Indian *curry* is famous around the world. People go to the market to buy the vegetables and the **spices** to make many different kinds of *curry*.

The Himalayan Mountains are very high.
The tops are always covered in snow.

Dear Alex,

The Himalayan Mountains are in north India. The weather is cooler here. In the summer people move to the mountains. They get away from the heat, and they find food for their animals.

Love,

Robert

P.S. Dad says that the highest peak in India is called Nanda Devi. It is 25,645 feet or 7,800 meters above the sea.

People can buy hot food when a train
comes in to a station.

Dear Maria,

Most people in India do not have cars. Many people here travel by bus or by train. We went on a train to the city of Calcutta. The train was very hot and crowded.

Love,

Carmen

P.S. Mom says that in the countryside people often ride on carts that are pulled by two **bullocks**. Farmers use the carts to carry vegetables and wheat to sell at the market.

A busy street in Calcutta

Dear Alan,

Calcutta is the biggest city in India. It is on the east coast. We stayed here with my cousin Sita. She took us to the market to buy presents. We saw many poor people there.

Your friend,

Sanjay

P.S. My cousin is eight years old. She goes to school like us. Sita says that many children here do not go to school. They have to go to work instead.

A painting in the Ajanta caves

Dear Meg,

Lots of **tourists** come to see these cave paintings near Aurangbad. They were painted by people who lived in India more than 1,000 years ago.

Love,

Ruth

P.S. The weather here is very hot. Dad says that we are near the **tropics**. The only rainfall is when the **monsoons** come. These rains come once a year at the end of July.

Making a film in Bombay

Dear Nick,

You would love Bombay. People call it India's **Hollywood**. More films are made in Bombay than in any other city in the world. Indian films are shown in many countries.

Your friend,

Craig

P.S. Bombay is on the west coast of India. Mom says that it is a very important city. There are big office buildings and hotels. Lots of people come to Bombay to find work.

The *Parami Haveli* palace, Hyderabad at night

Dear Tom,

We are staying in Hyderabad. There are many tourists here. We went to see this beautiful old building. It is called the *Parami Haveli*, which means the Old Palace.

Love,

Andy

P.S. Tourists come to Hyderabad to see the old buildings. Mom says that Hyderabad is also a busy modern city. **Traders** come here to buy and to sell goods.

Fishermen on the beach in Goa

Dear Sally,

Now we are on the west coast of India. Lots of people come here for their vacation. Today we went to the seashore. We saw fishermen selling fresh fish on the beach.

Love,

Joseph

P.S. Dad says that the Indian coast is more than 4,000 miles long. The **harbors** are full of big ships. Ships carry goods from India to sell in countries all over the world.

Children playing a ball and bat game called cricket

Dear Tom,

People in India love cricket. Everyone supports the Indian team. Children play this game all the time. In every town and village you can see them playing in the streets.

Love,

Denise

P.S. Mom says that there are many tigers, bears, and other wild animals living in India. People used to hunt them for sport. Now the animals are **protected**.

Children at a festival

Dear Natalie,

These children are dressed in special clothes for a **parade**. It is part of a festival. Many people come to watch the singing and dancing. There are snacks to eat, too.

Love,

Todd

P.S. Dad says that most people in India are followers of the **Hindu** religion. Many festivals are held to remind people about important Hindu events from the past.

The Indian flag flying in Bombay

Dear Susan,

There are three stripes on the Indian flag. They are orange, white, and green. The blue wheel in the center of the flag stands for Asoka. Long ago Asoka was a ruler in India.

Love,

Linda

P.S. Mom says that Great Britain once ruled India. Now the people in India choose their own leaders. This kind of government is called a **democracy**.

Glossary

Bullock: A young bull

Capital: The city where people who rule the country meet

Democracy: A country where all the people choose the leaders they want to run the country

Harbor: A place where ships are safely tied

Hollywood: A town in the United States where people make movies

Hindu: A person who follows the Hindu religion. Hindus believe in many different gods. They also believe that people are reborn after they die.

Monsoons: Very heavy rain and strong winds at the end of July

Parade: Groups of people who walk, march, or dance through the streets

Protected: Looked after. The animals are protected so that they do not die out.

P.S.: This stands for Post Script. A postscript is the part of a card or letter that is added at the end, after the person has signed it.

Spice: Part of a plant that is dried and used in cooking to give food a stronger taste

Tourist: A person who is on vacation away from home

Traders: People who buy and sell things to earn a living

Traffic: The cars, trucks, and bikes that carry people and goods on the road

Tropics: The lands near the middle of the Earth. The heat from the sun is strongest here. We draw lines on maps to show the position of the tropics.

Index